THE HARBOUR

DIMITRIS TSALOUMAS

THE HARBOUR

University of Queensland Press

18·2.00

First published 1998 by University of Queensland Press
Box 42, St Lucia, Queensland 4067 Australia

Typeset by University of Queensland Press
Printed in Australia by McPherson's Printing Group

Distributed in the USA and Canada by
International Specialized Book Services, Inc.,
5804 N.E. Hassalo Street, Portland, Oregon 97213-3640

ISBN 0 7022 30812

Acknowledgments

Some of the poems in this collection have previously appeared in *World Literature Today* (USA), *Critical Survey* (UK), *Eureka Street, The Literary Half-Yearly* (India), *Metre* (Ireland), *Cimarron Review* (USA), *Heat,* and *Southerly.*

The sequence *Notes from the Cave* was first published in *Making Connections: a Festschrift for Matt Simpson* (Stride Publications, UK).

The sequences *Six Improvisations on the River* and *A Song of Praise* were first published as a pamphlet by Shoestring Press (UK, 1996).

Contents

A Summer House

Between the stone-pine and the cypress
the house stands, pensive under the moon,

shuttered against the fierce glare of the sun.
Sometimes, when the sea is a windy blue

and gold hibiscus tips stain the corrugations
of the cicada's song a scarlet red,

it seems remote as its beginnings and whiter
than any white you've seen before.

Five generations spent happy summers there
if the accounts of the poor can be relied upon.

Children grown dead in foreign parts have left
their voices, and if on a still night

you listen hard enough you'll hear the rattle
of silver and glass, the hustle and laughter

of people about their business of living.
Yet on its steps you never fumble for keys.

It has no doors, it wraps you like a thought
intent on its object, the shell of a psalm

that guards the kernel of divinity. No candle
burns there, nor urge for words: I nurse

no loneliness of place. But now and then,
between a falling star and the next, I span

the century, cut through its green of hills
and the plains of brass and fire to where I sit

and feel its failing pulse, its dead weight
of dross and ornament. I travel light now,

bring nothing back. The house is bare,
unfit to host fastidious guests.

The Second Journey

I

This then the rumoured region
of dust and stone
land of the stillborn seed

no bright star this time

we have travelled vaguely
by this beat of drums

sorrow roams abroad all night
irrelevant

a scatter of hoofs
footfalls adrift in the plains
under the leprous moon

night paths unfold
to days stark as theorems

come light, skin clings to bone
excluding flesh

II

Suspicion has crossed the borders
of our kingdoms,
entered the peace of our palaces
the cool of vaults.
A sadness has long since tainted
the angels' midnight song.
Therefore we journey forth
mustering evidence against the bliss
of our millennial dreaming.

We rode through lands of plague
and stench of famine and war,
acknowledged death that brings
but a renewal of desolation.

This sun has drilled a shaft
into the shadowed mind
forbidding private vision, even
the scarring lure of the mirage.

III

Maybe I heard their witnessing
maybe I saw them riding past
asked indiscreet questions.

Nothing is certain. Loathing
deceives the hiding self
fear dictates evasion.

No paean from heaven burns
no beckoning star
in the whorls of my memory.

Bones breathe the moan
of orphaned winds, drums hold
a far-off vigil. Nothing is certain.

I've been granted the freedom
of dreaming
denied the alibi of sleep.

Cowering in the troughs among
the shifting dunes one suffers
hallucination

no longer seeks faith in birth.

Daughter of Kálymnos

There, by the leafy window, the night
breathed warm. It brought me friends
and the woman I praise.

All day and through the night before
in the cicada haze of a far summer
noon-limestone hills

thrust up within my sea-bound mind,
up to the reckless climb of the goat
and the peaks of the hawk

that I might witness once more
the miraculous green of valleys hacked
from rock, the harbour hung

with balconies and loud with the colour
of fretting boats and Sunday bells.
Ah Kálymnos, Kálymnos,

mother of tough, sea-perishing sons,
your Dorian beauty has shaped
a daughter's love to haunt

my spendthrift days. You made me words
to welcome her, yet I've spoken none.
At her spare table I am but a guest.

Viaticum

Wearied with a greyness of years,
the leaden wisdom borne against

his plotting star, he'd left the road
and walked into a garden of waters

and gloom of moss. There was no stir
of wings, only a coolness at noon

under the Dog, a plenitude. Past dusk,
swans rippled across the breasts

of the woman. And now he bends
over her loveliness while poppy heads

lean on the window sealed with night
to kindle a glow on the perfection

of her sleep. May this gift bless him
whose path lies in a heaving plain.

Aubade for the Lady of Ships

On bastions torn off ragged night
shrill cockerel bugles declare
the day's intentions.

I lie alert
suspicious of my dreaming.

Yet peacock-proud the sun
spreads out a tail of majesty
above the levant hills

shreds from holy vestments
of emperors and priests
ripple to my shore

and I see you walk into a light
made perfect in the dark.

Soon there'll be wings and voices
in the harbour, perhaps a wind
in the rigging of your ships.

Offering

I have squandered my words
on substance less generous.

The house is poor,
I find no fitting gift for you.

But the small-leafed
round-headed basil on the ledge
is doing well this year.
It should last us the summer
though the water's salt.

I've gathered sage in the hills
and pennyroyal by the sea;
small camomile stars
and streetlamp traceries
through the window vine
on our dishevelled bed.

When you are gone
I'll hang them by the calendar
behind the kitchen door.

The Nightingale

Last night in our square of rubble,
on the stroke of twelve, a nightingale
was heard. And panic-stricken folk
leaned out of gutted windows
above lamp-posts that bent distraught
over the brinks of craters
wondering, bitter that such a bird
should visit in their grief with not
a tree, not even a spire to support
its crazy song.

A heartless hoax,
an aberration surely. And they railed,
they shook clenched fists and frothed
against the mockery. Whereupon
I laughed, and from the shadows cried
don't be such fools, brothers,
the song proffers no hope. That gift
you've squandered long since.
This is the hour of its perfection.
Be grateful to the bird that scores
the vastness of that loss.

So they began to wail, to beat
their breasts, pluck at the acrid air.
And I heard the keening
of Patagonian winds in the night lanes,
down shafts and corridors
and through the memory of pine slopes
and tall, drunkenly reeling masts
of storm-tossed Cape Horn ships.

The Rider

Send the snake away, hold back
the dogs, cries the rider from the gate

in the vast plain, rippling heat. She stands
in the doorframe, her gaze wakeful, fast

upon the rearing horse. A scorpion shines
pendant on the whiteness of her bosom.

Lady, I carry words that I must speak
in the peace of your house. I beg you

let me in. This fever burns, this journeying
has sickened my soul in the dead plain.

She turns as though weary of repetition,
bolts the door. The rider stills his voice.

This cannot be what I meant, he thinks,
shifting his gaze away from this page

to the wall. Must hang a picture there,
cover the cracks. Incorrigible, he spurs

the restive horse. He cries: I carry gifts
memory can't refuse; tinsel and rouge

of beauty grown old, charred wicks
of long-spent passion, resins and ointments

from royal tombs and scrolls of prophecies;
ashes from yet unburied cities: Lady,

I know songs that lull the insomniac Furies
and cradle the hurt of ghosts.

He stops, listens for echoes in the room —
nothing returns from the house in the plain.

For there, long since, I'd offered argument,
not incantations, gifts from the littoral

of trash-collecting age. The borders hold.
Trespass is in the loom of peace.

The Harbour

I arrived late one summer evening.
From a far parapet of hills
I'd seen the harbour and the ship
and window-panes ablaze
with the setting sun.
I was glad, for it had been
a long, lonely tramp.

I approached the town when dusk
was thickening to night
but saw no lights come on,
heard no dogs bark in the lanes.
Maybe there were no windows
or they'd been shut, made fast
against the flooding dark.

Yet I plodded on as though against
receding currents, drawn to
some centre, perhaps a boisterous inn
where there'd be supper waiting
and the warmth of straw.

But in the lurid light of the torch
I sat alone waiting,
thinking of the garden in heaven
and how it must be on the lawns
of that unending spring
with neither age nor fear of hunger,
nor loneliness.

Is there nobody there to tend
on a belated guest?

The torch reshuffled the shadows
and flickered one that bent
over the long trestle-table.
He sat, a gentle and thoughtful man,
his voice soft with sadness.
Nobody lives in this town, friend,
he said. There is no town at all.

You must be dreaming, I cried. I saw
the sun setting, the ship
in the harbour. What crude deception
is this? What childish prank?

He looked perplexed. Our truth,
he said with distant patience,
our truth is in another's fiction.
We are incapable of dreaming.

And suddenly he rose, his voice
a stagger of flame straining
to flee its candle in the draughts
of some wintry island shrine.
The ship ferries no passengers,
he said, carries no cargo. This town
is of no substance to the living.

In the Mirror of Candles

In the mirror of candles and shadows
a woman's stare fixed upon herself,

pale hand arrested in its grip
of a silk shaft of luminous hair.

This I noted long ago — a moment
of loveliness. But I never witnessed

the door's betrayal, the look of fear.
Nor did I hear the dragging scream

down the corridors to the dark place.
This too was long ago, beyond

the mirror's range; my records show
no loss. Against the years of famine,

the season of bloodstorms and headlong
calamity, I've built moments of stead-

fast hold, blocks of immovable time
to buttress mastery, to shore up gain.

Towards a Metamorphosis

As I come out of the burned woods
where I record the ashen hush of birds

and the fading tracks of the rain, I think
of you and know how much you matter

now that I no longer need your love.
The disinherited shall live in bitterness,

their tangle of root and stone loose
in the walls of crumbling cities.

What's written holds. Yet tenderness
avails my brothers nothing. Therefore

I'll teach you poison-words and how
to bare viper fangs and nail-carve flesh.

The Lords of Markets, soft with oozing fat
now strut abroad solicitous to lead

into the splendours of the nascent century
our diminished years. Hyaena-like, dear,

you will prowl the nights to howl and hiss
till they fear to sleep lest in the dark

your sisters rise and storm the hope
that fouls the dreams of their young.

The Shrine

Sometimes, before dark,
when the evening star frets pale
above the lingering brightness
that skirts an island's autumn day,
she leans on the windowsill
and gazes out to sea.
Not in nostalgia, not in regret:
her eyes hurt in the sun. The past
has settled about the house
like dust; it dulls the glow
of antique wood and brass. Her mind
wanders within the compass
of necessary things.

Yet freed from history
she now lives in a far place
by the harvest of youth,
where he's built a shrine for idols
no stranger comes to worship.

It's peaceful in the harbour.
The ships no longer sail
into the thunder of surf
borne on the winds from beyond.
No hustle of commerce ever crowds
the patient wharves. What is,
here he bends to his will;
her bitter truth's but fiction.

Towards the New Millennium

Like a prosperous unknown land
whose promise is a phoenix yet unborn
in the ashes of an exile's country,
the new millennium is now at hand.

Our reading of the signs can't be wrong:
seabirds wheeling above, the frequency
of flotsam, dead fish and tamarisk bloom
on slick-dappled seas, the odd discarded thong.

I was loath to embark. Till as in sleep
a rumble of multitudes from sinking shores
like an ocean breaking over the dykes of
remotest Australia fathoms deep

down the map of known lands; a roar
of blood rushing like a myriad drums
rolling to mutiny under the whirr
of great wings beating the night to soar

above the binding dark — had taught me fear
of loneliness, hope in tidal rips.
For dreaming stills in the haven of harbours,
life stalls, meaning's bestowed, unclear.

Rational vision firms our captains' grasp
of heaven's message, who now clearly bid
the soul remember bliss once hers and long
for home again. Wakeful, our captains rasp

precise instructions. Now and then, they scan
the line below the sulphur-acid sky,
study the smoke formations, speak words
we marvel at as at a new-born sun.

The rumble persists, but neither metaphor
nor simile will pin its shifting source.
Shall I compose a charm to lull the now,
a song of praise to welcome the before?

The captains, like the philosopher of old,
see just two points in time's compass, both
the same. Between, it frets and coils
and bites its tail to spring from either's hold.

Sonnet

I'd been looking for her vaguely
through morning mists, noonday haze,
and in the years of war and loss
in tropic islands rich
by the love of endless summer.
I had also looked in parts
less glamorous, the drab monotonies
of mule-drawn time.

So when she crossed into my lands
I failed the hope of expectation:
she brought familiar gifts. Now rid
of scope, my demands are minimal —
another dress, a new hairstyle. I
no longer goad the stubborn beasts.

Ballad

"What's the bird humming in the treeless land?
Why does the cloud spit on hissing stone?"

"Finch dawn and partridge dusk — the hoopoe
skittered drunk across our summer days …"

"It's simpler things I ask; I must break through
the bird's reserve, the stone's bitter spite."

"… and boats hooting loud from distant ports,
people waving on the wharves to waving strangers."

"Mother, that's as may be, but I must know
what stifles the song, drives the shiftless cloud."

"The bird's an orphan, son; it talks to itself.
Into the drinking trough the tap drips brine."

"I hear the drops, they ripple to rings my dreaming.
But where's the path you trod to bring me here?"

"Go find green fields and season-wise plains.
The stone is stone. It neither takes nor gives."

The Retreat

He left early last night,
walked out in a huff.
Yet dinner'd been satisfactory,
the conversation bland, the wine joyous
in its measured delightfulness.

Nevertheless, he left the house
protesting innocence,
although an icy stellar wind
swept through the desolate city
and the streets were dark.

O love never defeated in war,
how come this testiness?
When did you last retreat
before a battle was joined?
Appalled, we looked into our cups.

Then watched the news, talked politics,
yawned ourselves to bed. A creak,
a stealth on the stairs aroused
suspicion. Discreetly, I thought
of our guest, afraid of his returning.
She heard sleep's step of lead.

A Song of Praise

I

Faint lightning pulse
storm-blown shreds maybe
of northern lights

they uncover horizons
frustrate night's
cohesion

Sea-sprung
great serpents twist
in the fitful
illuminations

helmeted angels guide
multitudes
along the ridge
of jagged darkness

in the calm shallows
the harbour lights probe
prodigious depths

II

In the small hours
a rumble of armies breaks
into the children's room

lights come on
in the neighbourhoods

old people sit up
in bed

they cough
into glass bowls they drop
pearl-tears

the thinker's vigil snaps

because children
from tears grew leaf
grew fruit

great trees that spanned
blood-lusting squares

III

Now at the third cock-crow
pale-fingered dawn
betrays the creeping sun

silent crows beat
for the rubbish dumps
over the far hills

the smaller birds
sit in their balconies
scolding their young

soon in the schools of heaven
children will colour in
the sheets of sky and sea

Good morning my love
numb with the chill of dew
the snake uncoils

in the cool of streams
trout rub their bellies
on polished stone

IV

Come Muse inspire the poet
in his confusion,
release the fugal themes
coiled in the pliant ear;

let roses weep, graves
rejoice, churchbells announce
the Devil's evening walk
in our village square;

undo the knot of tongues
that politicians may sort out
the world's polyphony,
bare its counterpoint.

Harmony-ruled, time frets
and plods inevitable
for days and nights beyond
the might of number.

V

The sun is on his way to noon
the pavement melts

grapes languish on the stalls
strawberries gleam
sleek fish recline on marble

they regard the customer
through arctic mists

with knives back in rigid sheaths
butchers arrange red cuts
with sprigs of parsley
steady to a polished rest
bald heads and trotters
of pilloried pigs

a crowd gathers curious
they cross at the lights

peacocks and sparrows
the mighty strains of Bach
two butterflies
wobbling on crutches still
survivors of burned-out valleys

VI

Wrapped round the post aloft
the talismanic smile
the Candidate

people hurry past the Hope
of Future Generations

evil pollutes the streets
flows into basements
creeps up the stairs

great moths flutter about
in vaulted dark destroying
the Fabric of Society

as caterpillars crawl in mile-
long sections to the beach
along the city's arteries

siren-panic and horn fanfare

pubs drone in smoke and reel

Police with spiked truncheons
behind riot shields
move on the Garden of Whores

VII

The Low's serrated front
drags loops of turning winds
and towering puffs of rain
across the city's map

it puts a sparkle on cars
flushes dogshit down the drains

people sit to think
tear the tops off frosty cans

every screen lights up

vague suspicions flicker
of last night's phenomena
knives approach extended hands
beds heave as fitful light
flashes through naked glass
and bars of steel-shadow compel
the writhing lovers

revellers sing the new year in
the nursery bursts into cheers

Goodnight my love
across our rosebush patch
the trail of blood glows fresh
under each moon

The Garden

The garden is minimal: potted geraniums,
a honeysuckle, a raised bed of herbs.

It is a space of flagstone and walls
washed white, where I sit by the door

and listen to the sea below. Come summer,
I shift the chair under the vine.

At times reports disturb the harbour
of great events, and I cross the hills

eager for gain, despite past deception.
Thus I come back and sift the burden

of my ears, the clash of begging-bowls
and the wail of vagrant populations,

the clatter of armies marching to war
and moneylenders' invitations;

quarrels of whores in the market lanes
and vendors' Siren-calls. I sift

for grains of gold that will melt down
and in the moulds of this frugal place

shape such forms as carry truth beyond
the hard-edged regions of its meaning.

Some Observations in the Haiku Manner

I

Axe driving wedge through
dawn frost. The rooster next door
cracks open my day.

II

Rise early, son, learn
from blank skies before the blast
of gathering light.

III

A splendid fish leaps
into rainbow glory, flouts
a lifetime's dream catch.

IV

She came blindingly
like the sun who's never seen
a star in his life.

V

Woman with child broods,
hens scratch in cherry blossom.
The sun's in the tree.

VI

The drops of your love
took long years but filled at last
my cup with sourness.

VII

Pigeons by rainbow
fountain; the old woman sees
peacocks on the lawn.

VIII

All the light I missed
now burns in the flyblown eyes
of sad bone-children.

IX

What are the angels
up to? What's the song for in
a church up for sale?

X

Your daughter's blossomed
this year, friend, though green-soft thorns
may yet prick this praise.

XI

In the oil-lamp gloom
cobweb cradles a fly's husk.
I see no spider.

XII

Boats throb in at dawn.
Yawning, the village cats rise
and head for the beach.

XIII

Red mullet and bread
in the sea breeze — my woman,
tanned like muscat wine.

XIV

Glow-worms working out
my night like coalminers in
darkest Siberia.

XV

Your forgiving tears,
perfect like these drops of wine
I pressed long ago.

XVI

Ah Melbourne of my
youth, lovers sit eating cakes
down in Acland Street.

XVII

Stylite gulls on posts
navel-obsessed in rain all
day off Elwood Beach.

XVIII

Blue sea breeze sprinkling
with dust from butterfly wings
her dusk horizons.

XIX

I love you friend in
your coal-pit; it's those black nails
keep you from my table.

XX

Southern birds scratch the
cobalt sky, rip sheets of heat.
Gum claws score the wind.

XXI

Her voice candle-lit,
mellow now through a varnish
of rare violins.

XXII

Yes, mother, I smell
oil and melting wax and stale
ghost whiffs of incense.

XXIII

And you, dear sister.
The dog's sad, perhaps with age.
The house is kept clean.

The Quest

A romantic tale

They'd been on the road a long time
across plains and rivers, up slopes
of days loose with scree and forest nights
beneath star-sifting canopies of leaves,
then down a spiral rim of mists
that rose in convolutions from far,
maybe verdant depths. But the descent
was into stone and nakedness,
a plain shrunk to mean horizons,
evenings that stretched out vast
to a sudden fall of dark.

At last,
one night they reached a pass where
the sound of roused speech was heard,
and held aloft by trembling hands
a stormlamp lit the horseman's eye.
"Who are you, friend, and how many of you
are there behind this light?"
"Some kinsfolk, Keeper; a handful of friends.
I must find their place, take them home
to rest. Their sadness now's more
than I can bear." "I no longer know
the meaning of such words, or what it is
I keep," said the man with the light.
"Polarity shifts in these parts,
memory runs aground. But all the same,
when your companions flee their
rearing beasts, you'll know the place,
maybe the peace you seek."

So they travelled on till day and night
became one unchanging greyness,
its silence deeper than their own. And on
they went into the shapeless land
that lures the vagueness in the soul,
till they came to a wire fence
whose posts ran from infinity
to infinity, where by the ramshackle gate
an old man sat chewing a straw.

"I don't know how to greet you, Keeper.
We've come through uniform regions
of twilit time. Well met, though,
and may this be the blessed place
for those who seek a home."

The man by the gate spat out the straw:
"Been here since before memory. Nobody
ever sought a home in this country."
"It's my companions," said the horseman,
"I no longer can bear their sadness."
The old man pondered this, made a gesture
of vague amplitude.
"What I keep has no meaning," he said,
"You speak dream words.
This is unstable land. But ride on,
come through the gate if you wish.
I've heard of a place where chill winds
dry to dust the marrow in the bone."

So they travelled on into a vastness
of time without horizon
and lands of dust and cactus totem-stark
against an empty sky
till they came upon a rock where,
black-mantled, a man was squatting
as though in meditation. His dog
opened one eye and made to rise
but couldn't unfold its shaking legs.

"I must be dreaming," said the rider,
"I've seen you twice before."
The squatting man looked very sad: "Indeed,"
he sighed, "I forget. You are the one
who seeks a home for his people.
But the river's no longer here.
The border runs from North to South,
maybe from East to West. Can't tell
without a constellation in the sky."
"But I have a wife and children," said
the rider, "much work to do. The times
are difficult. Please put me on the track
you surely know." Still now like an idol,
the man in black spoke absently,
his voice devastated by drought:
"The living spirit is no help, stranger,"
he said, "no help at all. But ride on
since you must. I heard of a place
where the finch returns in the spring,
the nightjar ticks the space of darkness
under a sky of stars. Maybe that was
before, maybe it's in some time to come.
There's no direction."

And they rode away across the land
of dusk without direction
between the before and the time to be
listening for the finch, watching for signs
of night, of breaking dawn.
And there at last, sudden like a captive
sprung from the holds of memory,
a breeze brushed past the rider's brow
and there was a darkening in the air
and a vagueness of rushing waters,
of rustling leaves. In gladness,
he raised his arm to halt his people
and turned to speak.

But no words prompt
the sluggish tongue as I record this tale
of many years ago.
Maybe there had been none,
maybe he'd shaped them low and soft
that distance might mist their meaning.
Yet I remember this with clarity,
the bewildered stare, the halting hand
above a stone-stilled horse.

The Reef

"My life's but a reef," she said,
though like water seeping into the gloom

of wells, her voice had no sound.
"In the space between flood and flood

my time will never blossom into reality:
you shall have my body by that rhythm."

Strange sadness, this, he thought;
yet to that specious argument he spoke

sleep-words, spent since to a rustle
of leaves in the draught corridors

of memory: "Because imperious lust
flooded through me and I was drawn

into a cataclysm of drowning flesh."
I pondered this against the harbour sunset.

Restore words to their meaning, I said
to myself; the woman's reached a loveliness

beyond the ebb and flow of dreams.
Yet even as I spoke the reef was sinking

to a head of rock, to a plodding prow
dividing the treacherous surf.

And If She Turned Up on a Rainy Night

for Alex Skovron

In Bach's Great Passion
soon after the betrayal of our Lord
I heard the melismatic question,
What shall I answer my soul?

Pondering over texts whose words
are meant for music
to hang its yearnings on is profitless.
Yet it seems strange that one
should seek discourse with one's soul
in times of separation, as curiosity
compels the mind to the question
on this Good Friday and rainy night.

If they let me find her
I'd wash my hands, say I wasn't there;
and if she looked at me with a smile
I'd answer irony with irony, point
to the splendour of cathedrals,
the beauty of colour and ritual,
the glorious music.
Treachery's fruit belies its meaning.

And if she turned up on a rainy night
in my quiet room, when I looked
and she was sitting there
with a pilgrim's brown bundle
before this candle butt stuck in wax
since the blackouts of last year,

I'd forestall her questions, ask
where she was hiding in my need,
why this breaking of bonds with flesh,
this seeking alibis in freedom.

Fugal matters, these, no doubt —
voices entering bold, soon to get lost
in argument and polyphonic confusion.
But I'll say my prayer now
before the rush to resolution,
the major chord's implacable pull.

Six Improvisations on the River

for Djelal Kadir

I

Therefore, I sit in this room and hum the song
whose words I'll never recover. There's little gain

in tracing arguments gone wrong. Time invents
new premises, snags all conclusion taut:

snarled threads wash up in the hoard of the tides.
An orphan in the streets of ravaged cities

I beg, and in the wastes of slaughtered populations,
where the sickle glints and white teeth flash

amid the corn but nothing is given. Death's claim
is absolute in unforgiving times. Yet in a life

of equal seasons I have longed for the advent of
the spectacular even as in the forests of the North

I sniffed the soot of greasy incinerations and saw
the bloom of ashes on the wings of an ill wind.

And only last year, brother, when she smiled it was
the pleasant garden of spring and outside the door

my almond-tree stooped under blossom shuddering
like an angel bent over a sadness of lutes.

II

Tune of no substance, mere hum of seas within
a polished shell. But let the river metaphor dispel

illusion. For days now the bloated dead float past
my curious gaze along luxuriant banks,

water thick with pus and blood, nights filled
with strange dreaming. Thus in a dust-town square

I stand alone waiting for furtive step and burst
of blazing guns, guts quaking with fear.

I sip wine nursing old lust in brothel parlours
or, back from secret expeditions, I strut about

with strings of ears and bearded heads to cheers
from mine and my neighbours' kids. I talk tough,

find the river unscrupulous, swelling the city's
arteries, the harbour's drains. It floods the dead,

it courses down my veins and storms the sea to lap
the shores of continents and then, river again,

to steal below my balcony and leave Byzantine gold
of autumn sunsets, birdsong, moon-fingered thrill.

III

In youth I learnt the craft
of marble and stone
but built no monument for my love.
I chose not to blaspheme
for her sake. Instead,
beneath our bedroom window
I planted a pomegranate-tree.

I tended it through nights
of frost and times of drought,
brought it water more precious
than blood. Till it grew strong
and bore a single fruit that swayed
and glowed in its leafy night
like a lantern in the dream paths
of the Emperor's garden,
like a full moon just born
from island waters
at some remote nine o'clock.

Firm in its soil it stands
defying the drift of speech.
But the river demands repetition;
detail accrues to familiar plots
confusing the mesh of fact,
old themes return to claim
foregone possibilities. Thus,
she would have mocked my generosity,
thought my gift impermanent,
mean. And I turned to the stone,
built for catastrophe
and the sadness of ruins.

I kept the gift to myself.
Secret and only mine behind
tall courtyard walls
that my neighbours might not sorrow
for the barren months of my winter
nor envy its scarlet summer stars
and autumn pride, nor hear
its farewell promise of return.

IV

The river's never far from this place. It runs
like a patter of rain or the thunder of hooves
and I can smell the refuse on its banks, foe's
rotting flesh, the swamps. Indeed, sometimes
the house rocks like a boat and sleep's a blessing
of healing potions and dream-rescued words,
and there are nights when it veers and tilts
in dizzy loops, and from the jolts
that strip my soul of leaves I know the rips,
the clash with rebel currents racing back
to lost beginnings.

O river of loneliness like
no other, great politician of promises never meant
to be fulfilled, day heaves and breaks away
from the words that might bind this song
to your meaning, and I wake and by the light
of the kitchen window read again tea-leaves and
coffee-dreg formations and random flights of birds.

V

Sun-struck, the hens in the neighbourhood cackle
from triumph to triumph, woodpigeons spell

three-syllable words tricked into various meaning
according to the ear's disposition. Nevertheless,

higher up in the hills goatherds whistle
and crows take off grumbling in the heat

and your image comes unambiguous, untouched by mist
of memory or dross of fact. And so the music

grows deeper and sadder, brother, off the shores
of the Greek seas and the bone plains of Anatolia,

and the air is ashen, thorny with the smoke
of burning islands and ships. Yet far as I recall

you weren't among the slaughtered at Mykale, nor
a survivor at Yérondas, where from my rock I sailed

alarmed at the news, and from the hills of Samos
watched and cheered with the gathered population

till I was hoarse, urging the champions on to burn
and drown the grim armada. You came much later,

only the other day at dusk across the Ocean stream
to bring me news of fellowship. I spend my days

in fear of the lurking foe, unbolt the door
to coded knocking. These barbarians are no solution.

The blood seen dripping once from our tall roofs
seeps through to stain the ceiling, threaten my bed,

and daggers meant for treacherous kings cut through
the room's thick air seeking ambitious hands.

VI

But to the gold from Byzantium, the wings
at blue dusk and moonlight scales
quivering in mid stream

to fasten onto in quicksand times,
against the unison din of great hosannas
or deprecation.

Because, being river, it gives rise
to contemplation. Her auburn hair
for instance, upon the pillow at break

of day; a theme of larks and a riot
of nightingales the rising body and all
that richness of touch.

Or those who died the death of the torch
in a crowded square that light
might pierce the dark

locked in the vaults of the witness's
mind. These are facts, brother,
solid with presence

like the voice that brings glad news
to the stranger's place against the pull
of currents and the tear

of crosswinds. Being river, it never
stops. It irrigates and heals
entire populations,

it sweeps through tracts of bliss
where flow's unwelcome. And it carries
important information:

vigilant cities wait and nations fret.
But it resists interpretation, bared of
the binding spell of song —

words shelled and husked and cast about
upon the stream to grow the crust
of drifting meanings.

In the Front Room

In the front room
the visitors sit
in thick smoke.
They talk politics.

On the bookcase
the snapshot, now
yellowed,
no longer claims
attention. The face
unfashionable,
the hair too long.

In the kitchen
she makes coffee.
She thinks.
The politics of time,
of light.

Too much of both
maybe. Things faint
surely must retreat
in shadier places
than this house.

Back with the tray,
her smile agreeable.
Gently
she lifts the cat
off her seat.

The Bridge

I live simply within
a coolness of stark walls
although love's gifts
and ornament
are now sold at bargain-
basement prices.

Memory too comes cheap
in barren places
and in the troughs of time.
Nostalgia mustn't cross
the bridge I build,
the threshold of my house.

I often think of you
but it is out of thirst,
not sentiment.
You must have aged
whichever world
you may now inhabit.

Down along the shore
only the tamarisks weep.
Tiny finches stir
in the lace-trim foliage,
scatter the sand-grained
bloom. On delicate
branch tips they swing
in the fierce noon,
peck at sea-tears.

I build this bridge
to walk my soul. Slick-dank
and penguin-winged,
it'll never reach alone
the spring where love first
drank, from the rock's core.
I build this bridge
stone by stone.

Offering II

The music I seek for you
could not be rare.
I can scarcely afford
uncommon things.
But I'll build new harmonies
above known chords,
rhythms far more generous
than this, a gesture merely
of dubious reach.

The words you want to hear
are substitutes for wind
or hail, stone or star —
perhaps the rose that stains
with blood all loveliness
in dreams; for screech
and claw over flood plains,
or the white horse mane
tossing into the nursery
in some far dusk, prancing
on paint-fresh meadows
where no leaf stirs nor dust.

Let things be yours now.
Naming is for memory.

And stay the night.
We'll listen to the rain
gurgle down the pipe beside
my window, the southerly lash
across last summer's seas.
In the hush before dawn
we might see sparks,
hear the ringing blows
of hammer shaping iron
for ploughs to rip the land.

Mosquito Night

Images cross a throbbing screen.
Within the head, voices drone
inane repetitions. Mosquito night,
this. The brute has twice buzzed
my ear. Eyelids propped up
against sleep, I tense in the dark.
The hawk stopped in the air
that afternoon no more than six
feet above the bristling rock
and was still for a long time.
I watched him from the sea
hung in the wind on a plumbline.
Then he was gone. But now wild men
sit by telephones smoking cigars,
juggling computer tabulations,
poised to swoop upon and beggar
whole nations. Breathless, I pull
the sheet from my face.
The air is poisonous, the sun
strikes hard, but neither base-
ball cap nor breathing mask avails.
I roll onto the other side, wait
for the nerve-splitting whine,
palm by the pillow ready to slap,
squash the blood-mad thing.

The Rain

A wind rose early in the morning
and went level and taut through the pines
till noon. Then it brought livid cloud
and shreds of rushing sky. Towards dusk
the birds were blown about like rags.
The rain began later, sudden with thunder.
The lights went off.

And so it was
that the mains of heaven, by candlelight
and slow turns, opened to their full extent
and poured down on us a cataclysm
for long hours as we lay cowering,
fearing to leave our bed, and made love
more bitter than before. Whine and grunt
mingled with far tumbling noises, vague
lowing of cattle and shrill, torn calls
whipped by the wind against the panes
that bent under the pressure inwards
like liquid glass, screening monstrosities
that seldom leave the pages of books:
octopus-shaped faces, pregnant and serpent-
handed bodies and knots of creatures
streaked with rain and vanishing to come
again reshaped, recoloured in the dimness
of the diminished candle.

Groping for words
in the darkened room we prayed for sleep
when I heard a tattered, far cock's crow
borne on the crest of a squall. I spoke loud
then, I said listen, the day's at hand.
I've had enough of this, I'm moving back
to the harbour. Then I heard her voice,
slow and hoarse. The bird, she said,
must have misjudged its timing.
This rain's for ever. Then she fell silent.
But after a space her voice came again,
now stiff with thorns. Please make no plans
in the dark, she said. Your harbour's not
on any map. And it was indeed further along
the night, as I lay pondering her words,
that the bird's call, sure-footed now,
came through the dying storm and dawn,
lead-fingered dawn, crept up the ashen sky.
We slept.

Till suddenly the sun
reached the dividing cloud and crashed
bright cymbals of alarm. Summoned,
I sprang to the window and there witnessed
the devastation. The valley rolled
like a yellow river down to the shore
where no roof showed, no belfry nor mast
above the mud that spread out to sea
like an atlas region shaded for disaster.

I shall make some coffee, she said, prepare
the shopping list. But late that evening,
after the dinner and the wine and through
the smoke from chewed-on cigars I thought
I glimpsed the beacon at the Head, the ship
at its anchorage and the lighted wharves
under a sky that looked like rain.

Postscript

Regarding the matter of your wealth
my concern's as true as you might expect.
Besides, having none myself, I suppose
I can afford to pity the rich.
Your spendthrift sons will go
through the whole lot in no time,
to be sure, and your wife departed
long since. It is a shame though
that a life's passion should go to waste
in this way at your imminent death,
and you alone in the grand house
pacing and waiting without any hope
of compensation. Rather unpleasant,
I would have thought. But still,
it's best to take it like a man,
old friend. I would pay in advance
for my funeral, then I'd leave the rest
to charity for my soul's sake
and beat the taxman properly for once.

Last Visit

Fine Melbourne drizzle
by the petrol station.
I wait at tramstop 34,
think of him dying.

It was warm inside
the hospital. That summer
you held him by the arm,
clung to him as to a raft.

The tram is crowded.
A pale, long-fingered hand
clasping a handbag.
I daren't look up for fear
it's yours.

I stand, swing on the strap
to a nostalgic tune.

What bothers me's his cat.
Poor animal, hunched now
against the cold
outside the dark house.

Notes from the Cave

to Matt Simpson

I

I too have known the spin
into the vicious hug of iron,
held hard onto a fraying rope
against the outward jerk
into a howl of wolves.

Things from the scorching carnival
persist, the grinding music,
the stagger of feet.

I broke through spells and rings
of fire. Came back, each step
spied on by cockeyed masks.

II

Unlike yours, my people
no longer live in homes.
They inhabit a wilderness,
the corrugations of a harsh land.

They haunt this cave,
ride the sough in the grass,
the wheeze through siesta shutters.

Without gesture or speech
they gather in the dimness
trusting to invention.

III

I remember the children,
heads burning haloes
beneath streetlamps in the fog.

They are still there
in the fog.

                    Blue's infinitely
dangerous. Mustn't think
of harbours, stars hanging low
between a moonbay's horns.

IV

Time contracts. The horizon
gets closer by the day;
my people's whisperings
bounce back louder now.
They speak another tongue.

I lend them substance.
When the hour's propitious
I let them use my words
but record no message
within their meaning.

V

Ships sail past your window,
their rusty hulls.
I touch ropes, smell creosote
and tar, never question.

Solid with living, your people
resist addition.
They move in light hard as rock.

VI

Between Paros and Naxos
I too dismissed my shadow
one blinding noon

marble
nakedness, shudder of flesh
under wheeling birds.

Moth-like
among a flutter of shadows
it now circles the stone-light
testing its truth.

The Prodigy

My son was a prodigy. At three
he could speak and write
two languages; at seven,
recite in Homer's own tongue
the Catalogue of Ships.

What a child, my neighbours
would say, how proud you must feel,
and they would spit about him
to ward off the evil eye.

He sailed through science
in his youth, both natural
and metaphysical, explored the rise
of evil in the world,
mastered the secrets of prediction.

Your son was born a saviour,
my neighbours would say, crossing
themselves, blessing the woman
who gave him birth.
He's destined to great things,
we'll be the richer for his gifts.

Then suddenly he felt the pull
of other rhythms, heard calls
of voices yet unformed.
Feeling the challenge of things
imponderable, he turned to music
soul and purse.

I bear him no grudge
for the let-down, the bitterness
of it; it's my neighbours' taunts
I have to endure.

A jack of all trades, they sneer,
a good for nothing, really.
We saw this coming all along.
But you've got but yourself to blame,
filling his head with bubbles,
his breeches with wind.
He's taken off all right, helped
all the way by good taxpayer's dough
that'll blow out the deficit
and leave us begging our bread.

Autumn Days 1995

I

Waterfalls crash with sudden roar
into the craters of speech

Angels (of Peace) with ears set back
rip through the panic-struck skies
to punish rebel nations.

Tonight Venus may fall
within the blunted horns of the moon.

Solemn voice and colour shall back
the boasting of the just.

II

The man slumps over the wire,
shirt sunk in a mash of blood
and savaged flesh.

The head hangs on the other side.
Probably not. Can't make out
the label of his jeans.

Men with cigarettes to their lips
carry the dead off the pavement
leaving their shopping on the ground.

The blood's a shade too loud,
unnatural. Like pools of raw paint.
Could be the snow in the ditch.

Black-kerchiefed women gape
as if about to say something.

III

The moon's about to set
restoring light to action
in the northern regions of the sky.
Draco creeps back between to part
the tumbling Bears and turns
surprised his triangular head
on stalking Hercules.

It is the hour before dawn
when grey thought deadens the stir
in the flesh, scratches old scars
back to raw tenderness.

The frog gasps in the ditch
stilled by vague fears: the rustle
in the grass, the insomniac snake.

From the neighbourhoods,
the farthest corners of the earth,
a murmur builds up to the buzz
of a thousand flies pressing
against the eardrums from within,
packing a shell for thunder.

IV

Brief autumn storm, enough
to wash the sand clean of fag ends,
the trees of dust. They shine now
as the sun slants westward
and the seaweed tang's in the air.

The cicada's been silent
this year. The spirit hugs
the ground. At times, in the glow
of some domestic felicity,
jaçana-like it walks
on fallen leaves upon the waters
of tropical ponds.

Thus in the neatness of the humble
like a poor relation among
important guests, beauty returns,
moves timidly about the house
then wanders off down the lane
to the beach and beyond,
to slopes where the white of houses
flutters through the vine.

V

It brings dew from the west.
The ancients called it Zephyr,
a summer wind that trespasses
on autumn grounds.
It moistens roofs and vegetation
and breathes a balm of herbs.

Evenings ring vaguely sad
with sparse voices far off
and random goatbell clusters
dropping like handfuls of beads
into the opal sea.

At about this hour the oil lamp
is seen to flicker through glass
in Our Lady's shrine in the rocks,
as the fishing boats come in
and dark birds beat in the long-
drawn afterglow that haloes
the island sunset hills.

VI

The crack in the Patmian cave
no longer speaks. The Vision now
inhabits the world.

Deep in the well of history
there's a pulse to the dark.
The visitor who struck a match
would take in splendour and pomp,
the glistening gore and the exodus
of populations,
the squalor of glorious cities.

The narrow day far up at the mouth
of the well fans out projections
to shape the statesman's course.

Old themes persist in variation,
spun in the throbbing light
of stars long dead.

VII

The skies are screaming again
with a traffic of angels.
Indifferent, they carry out
precise commands.

Light explodes in the mind
splintering glass

tidal tremors surge,
smash past the Richter scale
storming the sinews unawares,
washing over loose flesh.

Proteus-like, truth scorns
the reasoned word. It is stone
polished in mountain streams,
axe in the shed. Often,
it's blackbird song on the fence,
merest rattle in a throat
imperfectly stuck;

snake of fire now, hissing
across landscapes of dereliction,
making good its escape
under the grinning moon.

VIII

My sleep creaks with ramshackle carts
rolling into the city their load
of eager witnesses.

Burghers and peasants, cowled monks
and men-at-arms crowd the space
between cathedral and glow
of immolation.

Ladies come to windows
above the wintry Roman square,
return to gossip and refreshments.
The spectacle below's been boring
enough. Brother Giordano is stubborn,
dying on slow fire a long time,
refusing to give satisfaction.

By nightfall, Jesus had spat out
the bitter core of his truth.
In Campo de' Fiori, they take down
platforms and scaffoldings.

Whiffs of smoke still rise
into the frosty air.
The crowds disperse, a pungent
sweetish smell clings to their coats.

IX

In the squalid ward
the blinded hope in the taut darkness
of plaster and gauze,
the scorched breathe plaintively
rigid in mummy bands.
Most awake feeling for limbs
scattered about in the streets.

Antique pipework provides decor
on the greenish walls. Some stains
are in the shape of islands
fringed with runnels of rust.
It could be anything,
the buckets are a fearful sight.
A smell of meatworks fouls the air.

The camera cuts to the child.
She sits alone, her eyes huge,
fixed on things the walls exclude.
They detach themselves, float free
untrammelled by discipline of lesson
or decoration. In the night they haunt
the litanies of great sorrow, drive
lament and flagellation.

X

Who guards the signposts on the horizon?
Are the winds safely hinged
on the axis of the compass,
the wheel of fate fixed on the Earth's?
Where is the point of separation
between night and day?

I have my thoughts but dare not subject
myself to scrutiny in full assembly.
Our sages' knowledge is vast
but their minds are spiked with thorns,
sprung with traps.
I fear the rules of this deadly game.

Does God's wisdom come by day or by night?
And does the earth tremble with its coming
or does it walk on Christmas snow,
on blossom-soft paths in child-sleep?

I stood at windows scanning the streets
for new phenomena, the sky for signs.
Nothing is as it shouldn't be.
And if it comes in war, no shopper betrays
acknowledgment, no market crowd can hear
its distant rumblings.

XI

Anaximander thought the Earth
floats in matter made of beginnings
and dissolutions.

                                        There's no disputing
this fact. But then he turned round
and hung it like a cylinder
in the dead centre of things
where nothing invites precipitation.

Opinion here conflicts. Some contend
the Earth's a globe held on a string,
a mere balloon.
Gravity's far too complex a thing
to set against simplicity
or to invoke against disaster.

Therefore swing it gently, child.
Don't let a sneeze,
a spiteful fly or sudden cock's crow
disrupt your reverie.

Praying to an Old Ikon

for George Konstantis

Your gaze breaks through
the dark-brown skin of centuries,
wanders in space beyond the rule
of time or season.

Lady of moon-drawn seas

This is the time of year
when bilious Scorpio lies low
in the southern sky
blowing leaves and dust
between doormat and wall,
blasting all day with desert grit
the landward gates.

Your eyes reach soft beyond
consolation, hands folded still
by the burning candle.
You are the blood in the rose,
the sap in the tree they turn
to acid rain.

I'd have you rest your head
on my lap, dream up a star
for drifting ships
on storm-dark waters.
Maybe I'd hum a tune.
But it is only rooks in the air,
sometimes a sudden sparrow.
I haven't seen a skylark climb
its vertical song in a long time.

Lady of moats and battlements
there is a sadness in the room

The Emperor's army rattles back
to winter quarters;
bottleflies swarm in the lanes.
The plague will hatch in the spring.

May the walled-in city guard
your people and every living thing
from further desolation.

NOTES

The sequences "Six Improvisations on the River" and "Autumn Days 1995" were occasioned by two of the many acts of great violence in recent history, the ghastly Rwanda massacres and NATO's onslaught on the Serbian-held territories in Bosnia, respectively. The first was begun and finished when the horror had settled to a set of haunting impressions; the second was born of the immediacy of its impact on the consciousness. Not that this particular action was more violent or destructive than, say, the Gulf War; but on this occasion I happened to be relatively close to it on my native island, and the strange blend of violence and beautiful autumn weather induced the kind of mood that seeks in poetry an antidote to one's oppressive sense of desolation.

Mykale (p.49), on the Anatolian coast opposite Samos, where in the summer of 479 BC the Greeks destroyed what was left of the Persian fleet soon after the battle of Plataea.

Yérondas or *Gérontas* (p.49), also in Asia Minor opposite Samos. In those waters, in August 1824, a mighty Ottoman armada on a punitive expedition against that island was destroyed by the fire ships of the much smaller but far less cumbersome fleet of the insurgent Greeks under the legendary Miaoulis. This is generally thought to have been the biggest naval action of the Greek War of Independence.

These poems were written between 1993 and 1996, with the exception of "And If She Turned Up on a Rainy Night" and "The Reef", written later to replace two pieces thought to belong more appropriately in another group of poems I was working on at the time. Generally, the poems are given in the order of their composition.